MW00909952

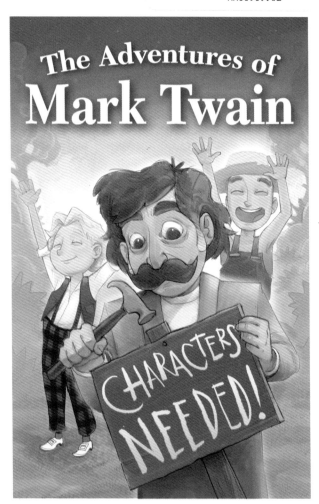

The Adventures of Mark Twain

By Darlene P. Campos, M.F.A.
Illustrated by Tom Bonson

Publishing Credits

Rachelle Cracchiolo, M.S.Ed., *Publisher*
Conni Medina, M.A.Ed., *Editor in Chief*
Nika Fabienke, Ed.D., *Content Director*
Véronique Bos, *Creative Director*
Shaun N. Bernadou, *Art Director*
Noelle Cristea, M.A.Ed., *Senior Editor*
John Leach, *Assistant Editor*
Jess Johnson, *Graphic Designer*

Image Credits

Illustrated by Tom Bonson

Library of Congress Cataloging-in-Publication Data

Names: Campos, Darlene Priscilla, author. | Bonson, Tom, illustrator.
Title: The adventures of Mark Twain / Darlene P. Campos, M.F.A. ;
    illustrated by Tom Bonson.
Description: Huntington Beach, CA : Teacher Created Materials, [2020] |
    Includes book club questions. | Audience: Age 13. | Audience: Grades
    4-6.
Identifiers: LCCN 2019031487 (print) | LCCN 2019031488 (ebook) | ISBN
    9781644913680 (paperback) | ISBN 9781644914588 (ebook)
Subjects: LCSH: Readers (Elementary) | Twain, Mark, 1835-1910--Juvenile
    fiction. | Authorship--Juvenile fiction. | Characters and
    characteristics in literature--Juvenile fiction.
Classification: LCC PE1119 .C325 2020 (print) | LCC PE1119 (ebook) | DDC
    428.6/2--dc23
LC record available at https://lccn.loc.gov/2019031487
LC ebook record available at https://lccn.loc.gov/2019031488

5301 Oceanus Drive
Huntington Beach, CA 92649-1030
www.tcmpub.com

ISBN 978-1-6449-1368-0

Printed by 51250
PO 10851 / Printed in USA

Table of Contents

CHAPTER ONE

My Name Is
Actually Samuel

Hello there! I'm Mark Twain, but that is not my real name. My real name is a spoonful of syllables—it is Samuel Langhorne Clemens. Some writers, like me, use a pen name when they write. Since my real name is longer than a yardstick glued to another yardstick, I made myself a pen name. I got my pen name from riverboat lingo. *Mark twain* means "the water is at least 12 feet deep, and a riverboat can float steadily and safely."

But that's enough about me and my name. I told you I am a writer. I love creating stories for people to read. A couple of years ago, my friend Charles Dudley Warner and I wrote a book together called *The Gilded Age*. However, that book was for adults. Now, I want to write something different, like a story about adventures—a story for people your age.

Unfortunately, my imaginative mind has been plagued with a serious case of writer's block. Writer's block is when a writer just can't think of what to write next. And trust me, it's torture. I wish characters could just stroll into my house and tell me about themselves. Having characters around me would make this writing process a lot easier.

Do you know what else is frustrating? There is no book about how to find a good idea for a new story. You can't go to a store and buy a good idea either. The wonderful thing about ideas is they are free, but, boy, sometimes finding one is as hard as squeezing an elephant

into a mouse hole.

One morning, I woke up early. I sat on the porch to observe the world around me. Sometimes, I can get inspiration for an entire story by just looking at a bird, or clouds, or people on the street. But as I sat on my porch, with gusts of wind rustling the edges of my papers, I didn't write one word. The birds in the trees weren't interesting, the clouds looked the same as they always did, and there weren't any people outside.

I suddenly had an idea—not for a story but for how to find an idea. I got a piece of a wood and a sharp stick, and I carved the words "Characters Needed: Please visit Mark Twain's house." I put the sign about a mile up the road from my house. I hoped some characters would see it soon.

CHAPTER TWO

Tom and Huck

You'll never believe what happened three days after I left that sign on the road. I was just sitting down to eat my breakfast when I heard thunderous pounding at my door. I dashed to the door and peeked through the peephole. I saw two boys who looked to be about 12 years old. I swung the door open, excited to see whether these would be the characters to inspire my new story. One of the boys was shoeless, dressed in tattered overalls and a straw hat. The other boy wore expensive checkered pants, a white button-down shirt, a navy vest, and shoes that shined like a light bulb.

"Good morning, Mr. Mark Twain," the one in the raggedy clothes said. "My name is Huckleberry Finn."

"I'm Tom Sawyer," the boy in the extravagant clothes said. "We were having one of our adventures when we saw your sign down the road, sir. But if you'll excuse us, we're hungry!"

They rushed past me toward the table. They gulped my coffee and gobbled my pancakes.

"My breakfast!" I cried out.

"We're your characters, Mr. Mark Twain. You don't even have to pay us. You just have to feed us!" Huck said, with a mouth full of *my* hot pancakes and syrup dribbling down his chin.

ɞ

It was clear Tom and Huckleberry, though he preferred to be called Huck, would make great characters for an adventure story. However, no matter what I said, they wouldn't behave; I couldn't get any writing done. Each morning, they helped themselves to my breakfast. This was followed by playing in my muddy backyard. Then, they'd run around my house, leaving their muddy tracks on the rug. After a few days of this nonsense, I needed to give them a piece of my mind.

"That's enough, boys," I said and shook a finger at them. They scurried around the living room, only stopping to make paper airplanes from the papers on my desk.

"Mr. Mark Twain, this is how we always act," Huck said and hurled a paper airplane by my ear. "You should be writing about our personalities, especially how funny I am."

"That's great and all. But I want to

write about real adventures, not just the silly mischief that you two get up to."

"Well, hold on a second, sir," Tom said, and he threw another paper airplane past my face. "We've been on lots of adventures we can tell you about. We've been all over the Mississippi River. We've seen and done all sorts of dangerous things. Oh, and I've got a girlfriend named Becky!"

Tom and Huck certainly weren't the kind of characters I expected. But I knew they weren't going to leave me alone until I wrote their story. I was still quite skeptical about writing a book about these two rascals. Oh well, it was worth a try to see what kind of story I could create, right?

So each day, I sat at my writing desk, pen in my hand and paper in front of me. And they watched, looking over my shoulders. They weren't much help. They'd rather argue about what should go in the book and what should be left out.

"Boys!" I had to shout over their

louder-than-fireworks-on-the-Fourth-o'-July bickering. "Do you want me to write or not?"

"Write about my girlfriend," Tom said, smiling. "Her name's Becky Thatcher, and she's more gorgeous than sunshine on your birthday. You've gotta put her in the story."

"Becky?" Huck laughed. "That's no adventure! How about the time we saw the criminals at the graveyard? That's *actually* exciting."

"You're just jealous I have a girlfriend and you don't!" Tom shouted.

"Boys!" I shouted again, but it wasn't any use. They continued to bicker about Becky, the graveyard, the Mississippi River, and which adventures and characters kids would find interesting.

CHAPTER THREE

Writing the Adventures

Obviously, I had a terrible time getting started on Tom and Huck's story. But thanks to their quarreling and mischief, they finally did something that gave me some direction. One afternoon, they asked me to follow them into the forest. We headed to the Mississippi River. I remembered playing on the river when I was about their age. As we admired the flowing water, I couldn't help but feel inspired.

"This will be the setting for my story," I said as I began writing. "Tell me about what you two did on this river. Did you swim? Float on a raft? Maybe you went fishing like I used to when I was your age?"

"We sure did. Didn't we, Tom?"

"That's right, sir," Tom agreed. He picked up a smooth rock and tossed it along the water. We watched ripples of water grow under the skipping rock—it was a mesmerizing sight. As I stared unblinking, I realized I had a story! I began to write.

"He's writing, Huck!" Tom shrieked. "He's writing our story!"

And they were right. I wrote and I wrote and I wrote.

One afternoon, I was in such a zone that I wasn't even distracted by their shenanigans. That is, until I noticed there was almost *too much* peace and

quiet. That could only mean one of two things. Either the boys had run away or they were up to something once again. I called their names…nothing but silence. I decided they had left the house. So I went back to polishing my chapter, or as some writers call it, *revising*. As I worked, I was startled to feel a poke on my back. I quickly spun around.

"Boo!" Tom and Huck yelled. They had my expensive white bed sheets draped over themselves.

"You boys cut my sheets?" I howled, clutching my hair in my hands.

"Oh, sir," Tom said and quickly took the sheet off himself. "You mean you still don't believe in ghosts even after we told you about the time we looked for treasure in a scary haunted house?"

"Put the petrifying haunted house in the story, Mr. Mark Twain," Huck said in his best ghost impersonation voice. (It did help that he was still dressed as a ghost.) "You gotta! It was exciting, and the readers will love that part!"

CHAPTER FOUR

A Short Vacation

Everyone needs to take a break from work here and there, and that includes writers. Writing takes a lot of mental concentration. After the frigid winter ended, I ran out of steam.

"My apologies," I said and rubbed my eyes with my ink-stained hands. "I'm having trouble paying attention to your story. I need to clear my head before I can keep writing."

"Oh, well shucks, Mr. Mark Twain," Huck said, and he gently patted my back. "Me and Tom will go on another adventure out in the country. We'll come back later, after you're all rested and ready to write again."

"Thank you. I appreciate that," I responded. Tom and Huck left my house later that day—after eating my lunch and running through the mud in my backyard, of course.

It was nice to have peace and quiet in my house once again.

Time passed. A whole season had gone by in fact, and Tom and Huck still hadn't come around. So I gave up on ever seeing them again. I reckoned I could write a good enough book without them, anyway. Then, one evening as I was revising several pages, another thunderous knock came at my door. I didn't think it was Tom and Huck. It was much too late for them to be out.

I stayed put at my writing desk.

"We're coming in, Mr. Mark Twain!" their voices shouted.

They burst through my door and sprinted to my writing desk. They grabbed pens from my desk drawers and pages from the book. Without speaking, they started to work. They crossed out entire scenes, added in new scenes, and wrote notes in the margins about how to add more sensory details.

"Now, wait a minute," I said and held both my hands up. "My book is almost done. You can't go and change it without asking me!"

When I said that, Tom and Huck rolled on the floor, laughing at me.

"Mr. Mark Twain, we thought you were smarter than that," Huck said through his snickering. "You think *you're* in charge?"

"Sir, you ought to know characters run the show, not writers!" Tom howled.

To be perfectly honest, characters do have a tendency to run the show.

By the next morning, I sat at my writing desk, listening attentively to Tom and Huck. They eagerly shared intriguing details with me about their latest adventures. They told me about an adventure with an angry man. They said he was obsessed with getting revenge on the people who had tortured him. I didn't think that was exactly appropriate for a children's book.

"Tom, Huck," I sighed and leaned back in my wooden chair. "I have a confession to make. This is my first book for kids. To be straightforward, I'm not so sure I can write your story the way you two are describing it. Do you think you should pick another writer to write this for you?"

"Don't be silly," Huck answered. "You were once a boy like us, and you went on wild adventures. You know it's not all fun and games. You can write this story—we know you can, right Tom?"

"You think so?" I asked. They nodded joyfully.

CHAPTER FIVE

Story's Finished

Numerous weeks passed. Each week, Tom and Huck's story got significantly better than the week before. We worked on the final chapter for countless hours. And then, after months of laborious work, I wrote "The End," and they cheered.

"My goodness gracious, we did it.

The story is done," I said and stood up from my chair.

"This calls for a celebration," Huck said. He and Tom rushed to the kitchen, loudly banging on pots and pans. After a few minutes, they returned with a piping hot cup of tea for me.

"We're not cooks or bakers, so this will have to do. At least until we learn how to cook or bake something," Tom said as he handed me the cup of tea.

"Well, tea is one of my favorite drinks. Thank you kindly," I said and took a sip. I coughed and spit the tea out. They laughed like hyenas.

"What did you put in this tea?" I sputtered out. They just laughed louder.

"Two whole cinnamon sticks and a half!" they said through their chuckles.

"You two!" was all I could choke out.

At last, it was time for Tom and Huck's adventures to reach readers.

The year was 1876. The people who remembered my previous novel, *The Gilded Age*, were enthusiastic to see what I came up with for my newest novel. *The Adventures of Tom Sawyer*, as the three of us agreed to call the book, hit the bookstores. I took Tom and Huck to visit one of the stores as a treat. Tom carefully picked up a copy, and Huck wiped his dirty hands on his shirt before he picked up his copy.

"This is real neat, Mr. Mark Twain. This is our story in a real book," Huck said as he flipped through the pages. "Thank you for writing it."

Tom and Huck continued to visit; but without a book to write, their presence was a bit too much for me to handle. If they weren't snickering about their newest prank, they were eating my food or tracking mud all over the house.

"Enough is enough," I said. "You two need to go home...and stay there."

"We promise to visit again sometime in the future," Tom said, and he shook my hand. "We thank you for everything, sir."

"Mr. Mark Twain, I just want to say thank you for writing our story," Huck said. "You told it so well that I bet in 100 years, people will still be reading about us."

"Thank you for your compliments," I said. "Be safe and stay out of trouble. Feel welcome to come on back—but only if you swear to behave better."

"We promise," they said in unison, and with sparkling smiles, they turned to go.

I watched them walk out of my house, into the distance of the woods under the twilight sky. I wondered whether I'd ever see or write about them again.

CHAPTER SIX

Back to Work

Time passed, and I did not write anything new because my concentration hit another obstacle. I tried going on a steamboat ride down the Mississippi River, thinking the beauty of the scenery would spark something in me. But as I watched the clouds over me, the bugs buzz past the water, and the magnificent trees along the river, nothing happened.

After the steamboat ride, I went home. I took my shoes off, stretched my arms, and relaxed at my kitchen table. Later, as I cooked dinner, it happened again—a thunderous knock on my door.

"Who's there?" I called out.

"It's Huck!"

I dashed to the door to open it. Sure enough it was Huck, shoeless and wearing the same scruffy clothes.

"Aren't you supposed to be having adventures with Tom?"

"We did, Mr. Mark Twain," Huck said and paraded inside my house. This time, he wiped his muddy feet on my clean rug. "As a matter of fact, that's why I'm here. You need to write about my adventures now."

"But Huck, I just wrote a book about you and Tom," I hesitated.

"Yes, sir." Huck sat comfortably by my writing desk. "And now, you need to write my book, so let's get started."

About Us

The Author

Darlene P. Campos is a young adult author. Her latest book is titled *Summer Camp Is Cancelled.* She graduated with a master of fine arts in creative writing. When she is not writing, she enjoys going to parks, visiting museums, cooking new recipes, and reading good books. She lives in Houston, Texas, with her husband, David.

The Illustrator

Tom Bonson loves to create characters who brim with life, color, and often a bit of lighthearted humor. From trolls and owls to surfers and giants, he has worked on a wide range of subjects. In addition to writing and illustrating children's stories, his work has also been brought to life in animated apps. He comes from a very creative family, which he credits for much of his inspiration. Today, he lives in his hometown of Bristol, England.